Dear reader,

ACCORDING TO "FUNTASTIC FACTS," THE WORLDS LARGEST POTATO WEIGHS—

FRANCIS, ZIP IT!

BOOK NOOK

I'M READING MAX & THE MIDKNIGHTS: THE TOWER OF TIME!

MAX AND HER PALS ARE BACK IN ACTION...

...AND IT'S THEIR MOST AMAZING QUEST YET!

HEY! WHY ARE THERE **TWO MAXES** ON THE COVER?

BECAUSE THIS BOOK IS A **DOUBLE DOSE OF FUN!**

THERE'S TWICE THE ADVENTURE...

TWICE THE LAUGHS...

POOF!

...AND TWICE THE MYSTERY!

?!

WANTED
FOR DEEDS MOST FOUL

A REWARD FOR HER CAPTURE

OOH! WHAT'S THE MYSTERY?

SORRY, NO SPOILERS!

WELL, THEN, CAN I BORROW THE BOOK?

SURE...

ALL IN GOOD **TIME!**

CHEERS!

MAX
& the Midknights
THE TOWER OF TIME

Lincoln Peirce

CROWN BOOKS
for YOUNG READERS
New York

Copyright © 2022 by Lincoln Peirce

All rights reserved. Published in the United States by Crown Books for Young Readers, an imprint of Random House Children's Books, a division of Penguin Random House LLC, New York.

Crown and the colophon are registered trademarks of Penguin Random House LLC. RH Graphic with the book design is a trademark of Penguin Random House LLC. Big Nate is a registered trademark of Scripps Licensing, Inc.

Visit us on the Web! rhcbooks.com

Educators and librarians, for a variety of teaching tools, visit us at RHTeachersLibrarians.com

Library of Congress Cataloging-in-Publication Data
Names: Peirce, Lincoln, author.
Title: The tower of time / Lincoln Peirce. Other titles: Max and the Midknights
Description: First edition. | New York: Crown Books for Young Readers, [2022] |
Series: Max and the Midknights | Audience: Ages 8–12 | Audience: Grades 4–6 |
Summary: Max's twin is public enemy number one, and it is up to the Midknights
to avoid looming dangers like trolls and pirates to find her before time runs out.
Identifiers: LCCN 2021028561 (print) | LCCN 2021028562 (ebook) |
ISBN 978-0-593-37789-5 (hardcover) | ISBN 978-0-593-37790-1 (library binding) |
ISBN 978-0-593-37791-8 (ebook)
Subjects: CYAC: Knights and knighthood—Fiction. | Adventure and adventurers—Fiction. |
Middle ages—Fiction. | Magic—Fiction. | Humorous stories.
Classification: LCC PZ7.P361 To 2022 (print) | LCC PZ7.P361 (ebook) | DDC [Fic]—dc23

Interior design by Larsson McSwain
Grayscale color by Tom Racine

Printed in the United States of America
10 9 8 7 6 5 4 3 2 1
First Edition

For Scout

Prologue

WHA-? WAS SHE A **WITCH**, THEN?

I GUESS SO... BUT WHY WOULD A WITCH TURN HERSELF INTO MARY 2.0? I HAD TO FIND OUT!

I FOLLOWED HER TO THE MARKET SQUARE. A CROWD WAS GATHERING FOR A SPEECH BY THE KING.

I GOT HER ALONE AND ASKED HER SUPER POLITELY TO EXPLAIN HERSELF.

AHA! AND THEN SHE PUT A **HEX** ON YOU?

NO... BUT THERE WAS DEFINITELY SOME FUNKY MAGIC GOING ON.

ALL AROUND, PEOPLE WERE TURNING INTO **DEMONS!**

1

"Ah! MAX!" Kevyn cries when he sees me coming. "You're just in time to experience my latest innovation!"

News flash: I have no idea what an "innovation" is. But that's one of the fringe benefits of hanging out with Kevyn: it really ups your vocabulary game.

He's beaming as he hands me a small square of parchment. "Consider this your admission to the scintillating world of READING!" he announces. Remind me later to ask him what "scintillating" means. Right now I'm more focused on this library card thingy.

"Whenever you want to read something, you merely show me your card in exchange for a book! When you've finished the book, you return it to me! It's as simple as that!"

It's Sedgewick, one of my classmates from the Knight School of Byjovia. He's also sort of the newest member of the Midknights—not that I've officially invited him or anything. What would I say?

"WANT TO JOIN OUR BAND OF *ADVENTURERS?*"

Nope, that sounds way too dorky. I mean, I THINK he'd say yes, but sometimes it's pretty tough to guess how Sedgewick feels about . . . you know . . . stuff.

PEOPLE ARE TOUGHER TO READ THAN **BOOKS**.

KEVYN, "MAX & THE MIDKNIGHTS" WAS A GREAT STORY!

YOU'RE TOO KIND, OLD BEAN!

"How's work on the sequel going?" I ask.

"Swimmingly!" Kevyn gushes. "I've very nearly reached the thrilling conclusion!"

Shocking? For once in his life, Kevyn might have picked the wrong word.

My stomach turns somersaults as I picture the girl I dueled in the market square. There's no doubt she's my sister. But I have so many questions.

"Er . . . no thanks, Kevyn," I tell him. "I've changed my mind."

I decide to take a walk and clear my head. But my thoughts keep landing on Mary. It's been over a week since she and I came face to face.

WHY HAVEN'T I **LOOKED** FOR HER?

Duh. Because I'm not sure if I WANT to. I've spent ten years as the adopted niece of a musically challenged troubadour. It's kind of a goofy life, but it's MY life. I like it the way it is.

AM I READY TO SHARE IT WITH SOME SORT OF **MAX WANNABE ?**

Without realizing it, I've been heading steadily toward the castle. A familiar figure leaps from the shadows as I approach the front gate.

HALT! WHO GOES THERE?

SEYMOUR?

SEYMOUR! WHAT A COINKYDINK! THAT'S **MY** NAME, **TOO!**

SEYMOUR, IT'S **ME!** MAX!

OH, **HO!** MY APOLOGIES, MAX! I GOT CARRIED AWAY!

IT'S JUST REALLY FUN TO SAY STUFF LIKE "WHO GOES THERE?" AND "NO, WE DON'T HAVE A PUBLIC RESTROOM!"

"Since when are you a royal sentry?" I ask.

"Oh, I'm not," he answers. "I'm just testing a new magical invention: MAL-WEAR!"

I walk down a long hallway and push open the golden door to the throne room. King Conrad is there. So is Sir Gadabout, the head of the royal guard. And the big-nosed guy tuning up his lute is my uncle Budrick.

King Conrad gives me a warm smile. Either he's happy to see me, or he's really glad the song is over. Probably both.

"Hello, Max!" he says. "What's on your mind?"

It's tough to decide where to begin, but I've gotta start somewhere. "Uh . . . remember how you sent Sir Gadabout on a mission to search for . . . y'know . . . my look-alike?"

He nods. "The mysterious Mary. Yes, I remember."

"No, not at all," he answers. "You'd always been an orphan and an only child as far as we knew."

"We had no cause to believe differently," Gadabout agrees, reaching into a pouch at his belt.

...UNTIL **THIS** CAME ALONG!

He's holding the locket he showed me last week—the one with Mary's picture in it. Which reminds me of another question:

WHERE'D YOU **GET** THAT?

"The tale behind it," Gadabout replies, "is a modest one, I'm afraid. No fire-breathing dragons or wizards or magical spells."

CARE TO LIVEN IT UP WITH SOME **MUSIC?**

PLUNKA PLINKY PLUNK

MAYBE NEXT TIME.

"It started perhaps a month ago," Gadabout begins.

I'D LEARNED OF A SERIES OF ROBBERIES ON THE OUTSKIRTS OF BYJOVIA.

IT WASN'T MONEY OR VALUABLES BEING STOLEN, HOWEVER. IT WAS **FOOD**.

I SENT ALVA OF THE PALACE GUARDS TO INVESTIGATE.

AND AFTER SEVERAL DAYS OF LOOKING...

...SHE HAPPENED UPON A THEFT IN PROGRESS!

CAN'T WE STEAL SOMETHING BESIDES **BROCCOLI?**

LOOK, I KNOW IT TASTES LIKE RANCID ROADKILL...

...BUT IF WE'RE TOO CHOOSY, WE'LL **STARVE**.

YOU THERE! STOP!

I ARREST YOU IN THE NAME OF THE **KING!!**

THE TWO ROBBERS RAN. ALVA GRABBED HOLD OF THEM...

...BUT THEY BROKE AWAY AND ESCAPED INTO THE FOREST.

ONLY THEN DID ALVA REALIZE SHE'D PULLED A **LOCKET** FROM THE TALL THIEF'S NECK!

SHE BROUGHT IT TO US, AND... WELL, YOU KNOW THE REST.

SO ONE OF THOSE CRIMINALS WAS **MARY**?

WE DON'T KNOW, MAX.

IT WAS TOO DARK FOR ALVA TO SEE THEIR FACES.

"She did hear them SPEAK, though," King Conrad adds. "She said they had distinctive accents."

ALVA SUSPECTS THEY'RE FROM **KLUNK.**

K-KLUNK?

Uncle Budrick looks terrified—which doesn't exactly shock me. The man's afraid of NAPKINS. Anyway, I'm curious.

WHAT'S KLUNK?

NO IDEA. BUT SOME WORDS JUST **SOUND** SCARY.

LIKE "TOFU." HEARING IT MAKES ME BREAK INTO HIVES.

KLUNK IS A LAND FAR BEYOND THE SEVENTH SEA.

YES, AND IT'S NOT A VERY FRIENDLY PLACE.

I **KNEW** IT! MY PANIC VIBES ARE NEVER WRONG!

HOW COME?

"It's a closed society," the king explains. "Klunkins are extremely suspicious of outsiders."

Great. My twin sister is a vegetable thief from an evil empire. I can hardly wait for us to do some family bonding.

"Identical in BODY, perhaps, but not in SPIRIT," Conrad points out. "How and where a person is raised makes a world of difference."

Hm. I didn't think of that. I was raised by Uncle Budrick as a troubadour-in-training. What are the odds that Mary had the same experience?

It's like a puzzle that needs solving. Mary and I should have grown up together. Instead, someone decided to split us apart. Why??

"I've got to run!" I shout suddenly.

"Not WHERE," I call over my shoulder.

2

I go tearing out of the castle. Why didn't I think of this BEFORE? The person who might have the answers to all my Mary questions is only a few blocks away!

Mumblin's the most famous wizard in Byjovia, and he's at the top of the magical power rankings. Yeah, he makes his share of boneheaded mistakes—remember when he accidentally turned himself into a STATUE?—but he knows every trick in the book.

Yikes. A guy the size of a six-hole outhouse appears out of nowhere. And he's not here to invite me to tea.

"You've got nerve, you little wretch," he snarls, "showing your face around here again."

STEALING? In a heartbeat, I realize what's happening.

He grabs the front of my tunic with one meaty hand. "You m-might not believe this," I stammer as he hoists me off the ground, "but you've got me mixed up with somebody else."

Wow. A couple of knights on horseback rescuing a damsel in distress! Not that I'm a damsel, but you know what I mean. Anyway, how medieval can you get?

"You two showed up in the nick of time!" I exclaim.

"Your timing's not too shabby, either, Max," Millie says.

"Whatever it is," Simon jokes, "he'll never look at a salad the same way again."

"It's not permanent," Millie explains with a nod toward the parsnip. "Mumblin's been teaching me about snap spells."

"Wait, that's CHARLEY?" I ask in surprise. "Isn't he the wildest horse at the stable?"

Simon grins. "Not anymore! I've been working with him."

We all climb on, and Charley starts down the cobblestoned street.

"Drop me off at Shady Acres," I say. "I've got to pick Mumblin's brain."

"His brain NEEDS picking," Simon cracks. "It's overripe."

"Can we tag along?" Millie asks.

"Sure," I answer. "The more, the merrier. And besides, this involves you guys."

IT COULD BE THE START OF THE *MIDKNIGHTS' NEXT ADVENTURE!*

SOON...

SHADY ACRES HOME FOR AGED SORCERERS

SHUFFLEBOARD 3:00 PM

THERE HE IS!

MUMBLIN!

HM?

UH... HOW COME YOU'RE IN YOUR UNDERWEAR?

UNDERWEAR? THESE ARE MY SWIM TRUNKS!

I TAKE WATER-SAFETY CLASSES ON MONDAYS AND FRIDAYS!

"This morning's session was top-notch," he continues, "until I was asked to practice mouth-to-mouth resuscitation on Ulrick the Unkempt."

A few minutes later, we're sitting in the front room of Mumblin's tiny cottage. He changes clothes and joins us at the table.

"Now," he says, his eyes twinkling, "to what do I owe the pleasure of your unexpected visit?"

I rehearsed this in my head on the way over here, but now my throat feels tight. "Well," I begin. "I was wondering if there's a way you could help me . . ."

"For my whole life, all I knew about myself was that I was a lousy troubadour who wanted to be a knight," I continue. "I didn't think there was anything else TO know. But now . . ."

Mumblin smiles. "But now there is."

I nod. "Uh-huh. When Mary turned up, I started wondering why stuff happened the way it did."

I THOUGHT MAYBE I'D FIND SOME ANSWERS IF I COULD SOMEHOW GO **BACK IN TIME!**

SO CAN YOU... Y'KNOW... ZAP ME INTO THE PAST?

Mumblin forces another smile, but not the good kind. It's one of those "here comes the bad news" pity grins.

"Max," he says softly. "Were it within my power to do so, I would gladly help you explore your past."

BUT I KNOW OF NO SPELL OR ENCHANTMENT THAT WOULD ENABLE YOU TO TRAVEL THROUGH TIME.

I'M AWFULLY SORRY.

Oof. Mumblin's words hit me like a punch in the stomach. I thought for sure he'd whip out some sort of enchantment or magical object or—

Mumblin dashes into the kitchen and returns with an ordinary-looking grapefruit. He sets it down on the table before brushing it lightly with his fingertips.

"This may not work," he cautions us. "It's a simple matter

for the grapefruit to show us a friend. It's considerably more difficult to focus on a stranger."

Two tiny figures are trudging through a dense forest. Mary's in front, and following a few steps behind is a woman I've never seen before.

Mumblin strokes his beard. "I think not, Max," he says, peering at the grapefruit. "These two don't look like the larcenous type, in my humble opin—"

"SHH!" Simon whispers.

"Fantastic," I grumble. "So even if they drop a hint about where they are, we won't be able to hear it!"

"There are other ways to determine their whereabouts," Mumblin reminds me. "Let's use the zoom feature to search for visual clues."

He taps the grapefruit twice with his wand. The pictures of Mary and the other traveler grow larger.

"What do you mean?" I ask.

"Those are chestnut trees," the old wizard explains.

Two more wand taps and the viewpoint shifts again, pulling back until the two figures are tiny specks.

"It's like a snow globe without the snow," Millie observes.

Mumblin nods. "Indeed. And notice the horizon."

Mumblin lays a leather-bound book on the table and flips it open to reveal a map, its pages yellowed with age.

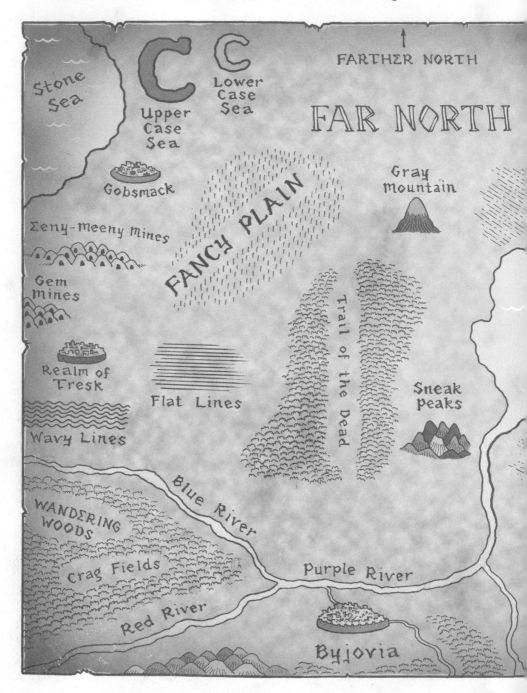

"Here is Byjovia, to the south," he says. "The Lion's Mane is north by northeast, a hundred miles as the crow flies."

Millie groans. "A hundred miles! We'll never catch them!"

"That depends on their destination," Mumblin replies.

"Gadabout thinks they might be Klunkers," I say.

"The word is Klunkins, Max," he corrects me.

"Can't you send us there magically?" Simon wonders.

With a sigh, Mumblin rises from his stool. "I wish I could. But my powers aren't what they used to be."

"That's okay, Mumblin," I assure him. "The Midknights will get to Klunk on our own. Without magic."

He waves his hands like a caffeinated crossing guard. "Perhaps I didn't make myself clear. I don't believe that you should go to Klunk at all."

"Why not?" we ask together.

"Because as soon as you set foot on Klunkin soil . . ."

KILLED? The word hovers in the air like a swarm of hornets.

"King Conrad and Gadabout told me that Klunkins don't like people from Byjovia," I say.

"Apparently not to Rotgut the Ruthless," Mumblin mutters.

Rotgut the Ruthless? Sounds like a fun guy. Just wondering—how come nobody ever calls themselves Nigel the Nice or Colin the Cuddly?

"Is he the king of Klunk?" asks Millie. Mumblin nods.

"How did you learn all this?" I wonder. "Conrad said that Klunk is a closed society!"

"That's true," Mumblin agrees. "But I'm . . . er . . . friendly with a witch who lives in a village near there."

YOU TALK USING BANANAS, HUH?

I USE A BANANA. **SHE** INSISTS ON USING A **PEACH**.

FUZZY RECEPTION?

IT'S THE PITS.

BUT I DIGRESS! THE POINT IS, MAX: IN YOUR QUEST TO LEARN ABOUT YOUR PAST, YOU MUST **NOT** JOURNEY TO KLUNK!

IT COULD COST YOU YOUR **LIFE!**

Okay, good to know. Not good in a rainbows-and-lollipops way, but . . . how would Kevyn say it?

THAT'S **ENLIGHTENING!**

Bingo. Finding out that some bloodthirsty king wants me dead is definitely enlightening. And you know what else?

Remember when I said that this could be the start of a new Max and the Midknights adventure? Forget it. I can't drag the rest of the gang along on some half-cocked road trip to Klunk. A knight doesn't put her friends' lives at risk.

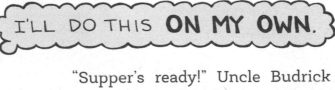

"Supper's ready!" Uncle Budrick says when I get home. I force down a few mouthfuls of . . . actually, I have no idea what I'm eating. But food's not really my focus right now. There's a question I want to ask.

"Uncle Budrick . . ."

"I didn't," he answers between bites of mystery meat.

"Yup," he continues. "When I found you in the church doorway, you were bundled up tight. After I loosened your blanket, I noticed a crumpled piece of parchment tucked into your hand."

"Parchment? You mean somebody left a NOTE?"

"It seemed an odd name for a girl," Uncle Budrick concludes. "But somebody wanted you to have it."

That's the million-dollar question. And finding my twin sister is the only way I can think of to answer it. I wait patiently for Uncle Budrick to go to bed. Then I toss some supplies in my travel sack and slip out of the cottage unnoticed.

"We knew you'd try to sneak off without us," Millie says.

"Because it's the noble thing to do," Sedgewick adds.

"It's not noble," I protest, feeling a little embarrassed that they saw through my plan so easily. "I just don't want any of you guys getting killed on my account."

Kevyn chuckles. "Max, you silly goose!"

THE SITUATION YOU'VE JUST DESCRIBED IS THE VERY **DEFINITION** OF ACTING NOBLY!

YEAH, BUT—

"It's no use arguing, Max," Simon breaks in. "You've saved all of our skins more than once!"

WE'RE COMING WITH YOU! LIKE IT OR LUMP IT!

※ CHUCKLE! ※ "LIKE IT OR LUMP IT!" BRILLIANT! I MUST WRITE THAT DOWN!

I'M COMPILING A LIST OF COLORFUL EXPRESSIONS!

SUCH AS?

"COUCH POTATO."
"BREAK A LEG."
"PLUMBER'S BUTT."
"IT'S NOT ROCKET SCIENCE."

WHAT'S A ROCKET?

WHAT'S A **SCIENCE?**

LET'S FIGURE OUT THE BEST ROUTE TO KLUNK.

Millie pulls something from her bag—it's the map Mumblin showed us this afternoon. She unfolds it on the ground, and Sedqewick examines it carefully. "It looks like there are three options," he says.

"What about option #2?" Millie asks, tracing a line with her finger. "Through the Fens?"

"It's a giant swamp," Simon replies. "Most of that area is under water."

"I suppose I should know this," Millie says, "but . . . um . . . what IS a troll, exactly?"

"I believe I can shed some light on this topic!" Kevyn declares, digging into his knapsack.

TROLL (f.e.)

Smaller than a crag but larger than an ogre.

Lives in hilly or mountainous regions.

Slow-witted, aggressive.

"We'll be okay, guys!" I say, reaching into my bag for my dagger. "We all brought weapons, right?"

We walk through the night and all the next day. It's grueling, but we have no choice if we want to catch up to Mary. Finally, though, we hit the wall.

"Sorry about that" Millie says, her cheeks flushing. "I'm still smoothing out the kinks."

"It could be worse," Simon notes.

I'm with Millie. Meat loaf candles sound like a goody bag gift at the world's worst birthday party. I lie down by the fire and think about the journey ahead.

"You guys have all lived here longer than I have," I say. "Any idea why Byjovia and Klunk are such enemies?"

"That's true," Sedgewick agrees. "King Conrad even tried to make peace with Klunk."

"He DID?" Kevyn exclaims in surprise. "I've never heard of such an undertaking!"

"Probably because it failed," Sedgewick explains. "I only know about it because my dad was a palace guard back then."

 IT HAPPENED BEFORE ANY OF US WERE BORN—ABOUT A DOZEN YEARS AGO...

 CONRAD KNEW THAT KING ROTGUT OF KLUNK HAD A DAUGHTER—PRINCESS EMELINE.

 SHE WAS SAID TO BE A GREAT BEAUTY AND HAD MANY SUITORS.

 AND SO CONRAD SEARCHED THROUGHOUT BYJOVIA FOR A YOUNG MAN WHO WOULD MAKE A SUITABLE MATCH FOR THE PRINCESS.

I'M THE STRONGEST, SIRE!

I'M THE RICHEST!

I CAN WIGGLE MY EARS ONE AT A TIME!

WAIT, WHY'D THE KING DO **THAT**?

I KNOW!

BECAUSE IF EMELINE MARRIED A **BYJOVIAN**, THE TWO KINGDOMS WOULD BE **UNITED**!

EXACTLY!

BUT HOW COME **CONRAD** WAS DOING THE HUSBAND-HUNTING?

SHOULDN'T THAT BE **PRINCESS EMELINE'S** JOB?

SURE, BUT IT DOESN'T ALWAYS WORK LIKE THAT.

ARRANGED MARRIAGES HAPPEN ALL THE TIME!

ARRANGED WHAT?

THAT WON'T HAPPEN TO **ME**, I'LL TELL YOU! I'M GONNA MARRY WHO I **WANT** TO MARRY!

ER... WHEN THE TIME COMES, I MEAN... *KOFF!* **IF** IT COMES!

BLUSH!

ANYWAY, **THEN** WHAT HAPPENED?

CONRAD FOUND THE PERFECT SUITOR.

SIR REGINALD WAS HIS NAME — A DASHING YOUNG KNIGHT AND BYJOVIA'S MOST ELIGIBLE BACHELOR.

CONRAD WROTE A LETTER PROPOSING THAT REGINALD AND EMELINE MARRY.

HE GAVE THE LETTER TO REGINALD'S SQUIRE, INSTRUCTING HIM TO DELIVER IT TO KING ROTGUT.

AND OFF THEY RODE TO KLUNK!

"I'm guessing Reginald and Emeline didn't live blissfully ever after," Simon jokes.

"Nobody knows if they lived at ALL," says Sedgewick.

"It will," I say, hoping I sound more confident than I feel. "Now let's get some sleep."

Sedgewick kicks a stone, dislodging it from the ground. He picks it up and brushes away the clumps of dusty soil.

"I have some bad news," he announces.

The night air suddenly seems still and cold as we stare at the ground around us. Kevyn's face turns the color of chalk. "They're SKULLS," he whispers.

WE'VE STUMBLED INTO SOME SORT OF GRUESOME GRAVEYARD!

...OR THE WRECKAGE OF A HALLOWEEN COSTUME STORE.

"Wh-what could have happened here?" Millie wonders.

"Here's a clue," I say, taking the skull from Sedgewick.

"Egad," Kevyn squeaks. "The Midknights are destined to become a five-course meal! We are in . . ."

"Let's think positive," Simon suggests.

"These bones look really OLD, right?"

In the moonlight, we can see it: a huge creature lumbering over a nearby ridge and toward our campsite. He lets loose another bloodcurdling bellow.

We grab our bags and start running. Luckily, we're faster than the trolls are. But we've still got one problem.

We scramble over a couple of rocky hills, and then I spot it, too—a weathered board nailed to a tree trunk.

OOF.

THE ENTRANCE SEEMS TO BE MAGICALLY SEALED.

YOU'RE SO RIGHT, DEARIE!

UH... WHO ARE YOU?

I'M WITCH EVRA! THE GUARDIAN OF BENTLEY'S PASS!

RROOARRR!!

WELL, CAN YOU LET US THROUGH?

WE'RE IN SORT OF A HURRY.

OF COURSE!

BUT TO BE GRANTED ENTRY, YOU MUST FIRST ANSWER A **RIDDLE!**

ER...WHAT IF THE TROLLS CAN ANSWER IT, TOO?

✳ SNORT! ✳ THOSE OAFS? THEY'RE DUMBER THAN A DONUT HOLE!

THEY'RE A FEW PEAS SHORT OF A CASSEROLE!

I'VE SEEN **SOAP** WITH MORE BRAINS!

CHUCKLE! THESE ARE ABSOLUTE ZINGERS!

ROARR!!

GIVE US THE RIDDLE, ALREADY!

OKAY, OKAY!

THE PASS WILL OPEN WIDE, I VOW, IF YOU CAN SOLVE THIS QUESTION NOW:

SIR KENNETH LEAVES GOBSMACK, TRAVELING 12 MILES PER HOUR. LADY BRONWYN LEAVES TRESK, TRAVELING HALF AS FAST. BOTH ARE GOING TO BYJOVIA, WHICH IS 88 MILES FROM GOBSMACK AND 35 MILES FROM TRESK. IF SIR KENNETH DEPARTS AT 10:00 AM AND LADY BRONWYN DEPARTS AT 11:30 AM, WHO WILL REACH BYJOVIA FIRST?

YOU HAVE GOT TO BE KIDDING ME.

I HEREBY REPEAT MY COMMENT FROM THE TOP OF PAGE 58.

WAIT! I CAN DO THIS!

ROARR!

$\frac{88}{12}$ $7\frac{1}{3}$

10:00 → 5:20

$\frac{35}{6}$ $5\frac{5}{6}$

HURRY, KEVYN! HURRY!

"I've GOT it!" Kevyn shouts. "They arrive in Byjovia at precisely the SAME TIME!"

Witch Evra beams. "Correct. Well done, lad."

We leap through the barrier and into a completely different world. Instead of dusty ground, there's a carpet of soft grass under our feet. Trees and flowers are everywhere. And the trolls are nowhere to be seen.

Witch Evra laughs. "Me? Heavens, no, dearie. It was here long before my time."

THE AIR YOU BREATHE IN THIS DOMAIN
WILL LIFT YOUR HEART AND CALM YOUR BRAIN.
BUT WHERE THERE'S SUNLIGHT, SHADOWS LOOM,
SO HEED MY WORDS OR MEET YOUR DOOM!

THE OXYGEN THAT SOOTHES YOUR SOUL
MIGHT SECRETLY EXACT A TOLL.
THE FRAGRANT MIST THAT FILLS YOUR LUNGS
MAY WARP YOUR WORDS AND TWIST YOUR TONGUES.

AND ONE LAST THING TO UNDERSTAND:
TAKE NOTHING FROM THIS MAGIC LAND!
FOR IF YOU CLAIM A PRIZE UNEARNED,
'TWILL BE A PAINFUL LESSON LEARNED.

Same here. In no time, we find a spot to make camp. Millie starts another fire—it smells like oatmeal this time—and then we flop onto the cool grass and fall asleep.

I wake up the next morning feeling tremendous.

AAAHHH! THAT'S THE BEST NIGHT OF SLEEP I'VE EVER **HAD!**

I take some bread and cheese from my bag and eat a quick breakfast. I kind of want to lie back down . . . but no, we should get going.

Sedgewick stretches like a cat on a kitchen floor. "Maybe we shouldn't go to Klunk, then," he purrs.

Hmm. Yeah, who needs Klunk? If we go there, we'll probably end up DEAD. Sedgewick's right.

I force myself to my feet. "Midknights!" I shout. "Snap out of it! Can't you see what's happening?"

It takes a mammoth effort, but I manage to get everyone mobilized. We start traveling east in a meandering line.

"Are you saying the rest of us aren't smart?" Simon snarls.

Funny, I didn't realize until just now how annoying his voice is. "No," I grouse. "You're putting words in my mouth."

"I am not," he shoots back.

I shrug. "Whatever. Let's keep moving."

"Don't pretend to be upset that Sedgewick's a Midknight!" Simon continues. "You're not fooling anybody!"

I feel the heat creeping up my neck. "What are you talking about?" I huff.

"Isn't it OBVIOUS?" yells Simon.

FIGHT! Seeing Sedgewick and Kevyn—KEVYN!—whaling on each other yanks me back to reality.

WHAT ARE WE **DOING?**

GUYS, **STOP!**

JUST **LISTEN** FOR A SEC!

THE AIR IN THIS PLACE IS TURNING US **AGAINST** EACH OTHER!

WE CAN'T STAY IN BENTLEY'S PASS!

BUT IF WE **LEAVE**, THOSE **TROLLS** WILL **DEVOUR** US!

WE **KNOW** THAT, GENIUS!

There's got to be a way out of this mess, but my brain's moving in slow motion. The air's taking hold of me again. It smells like sweetgrass and fresh fruit and—

"What do we need FRUIT for?" Simon grumbles in the most obnoxious way possible.

"To . . . call . . . Mumblin!" I say, as if I'm talking to a five-year-old. "He'll know what to do!"

"Yes, he most certainly will," Kevyn adds.

I lunge to stop him, but Sedgewick's too fast for me. He slips away, sprints to the tree, and . . .

PLUCK!

SOMETHING BAD'S ABOUT TO HAPPEN.

BRACE YOURSELVES, EVERYBODY!

HI. ME AGAIN.

TODAY WE'RE GOING TO TALK ABOUT **ADVERBS**.

WHAT? WHY?

• BRAVELY
• SURELY
• QUICKLY
• FRANKLY

"So . . . you're not going to punish us?" Millie asks.

"Oh, I'm ABSOLUTELY going to punish you!" Witch Evra answers. "The adverbs thing is only part of the process!"

"Wh-what are the other parts?" stammers Kevyn.

"Well, I'll have to expel you from Bentley's Pass, leaving you at the mercy of those big uglies from last night."

There's a blinding flash followed by a puff of white.
Then the smoke clears.

Whoa. Didn't see THAT coming. One minute it's Sedgewick standing there, and the next . . .

Evra nods. "Nicely said, girl. You've gotten straight to the core of the issue."

"I thought you were a GOOD witch!" wails Millie.

"Oh, but I AM!" she replies. "I'm good at LOTS of things!"

"I'm afraid you'll have to figure that out for yourselves, dear," she answers. "And I suggest you do it quickly."

Millie waves her wand over the apples, chanting quietly,

but nothing happens. "This isn't working," she groans. "Witch Evra's magic is a lot stronger than mine."

"You don't say," Simon snorts. "Listen, I have a REAL idea."

"Whose nose are you calling plain?" hisses Simon.

"BUTTON it, you two," I bark, kneeling beside the apples. "We're all on the same side."

There's a long silence and then a faint hum. Finally, a familiar voice comes crackling through one of the apples.

Witch Evra flicks her wand, and the first apple disappears with a loud pop. "Congratulations," she tells us. "You've managed to save your companion."

BUT GOOD LUCK TALKING TO YOUR **WIZARD** FRIEND USING **THAT**!

She twirls her wand again and conjures a large wooden door. It hovers in the air for a moment before settling on the grass with a thud.

"This will sound rather unfriendly," the witch confesses.

...BUT I MUST ASK YOU TO **LEAVE** NOW!

Hey, that's fine with me. This lady just made Sedgewick an apple. If we try to fight her, she'll turn the rest of us into fruit cocktail.

"I hope there are no hard feelings," she says as we gather our belongings. "I'm just doing my job."

As we cross the threshold, the door disappears behind us. That clinches it: there's no going back to Bentley's Pass now. But why would we WANT to?

Looks like Kevyn's thinking the same thing. "Midknights!" he blurts. "I owe all of you a monumental apology!"

> I REALLY "SHOT MY MOUTH OFF" BACK THERE!

> ME, TOO. SORRY, GUYS.

> WE **ALL** DID! IT WASN'T OUR FAULT!

> WE WERE BEWITCHED BY THE AIR OF CONTENTMENT!

"Well, we're free now," I remind everyone.

> OUR TROUBLES ARE BEHIND US!

> ER... THAT'S TRUER THAN YOU KNOW.

> RAHRRR!

Uh-oh. Here's where we came in—LITERALLY. But this time, the trolls have us surrounded.

"How does that help us?" I shout as the trolls draw closer. "Uncle Budrick is the only musician we know. . . ."

Our only chance? Then we're probably toast. I've got a voice like a rusty hinge. But I guess I have to take my shot.

IF YOU'RE EAGER TO VISIT, YOU'RE WELCOME TO TRY. KEEP YOUR HEAD ON THE GROUND AND YOUR FEET IN THE SKY!

I WON'T COMMENT ON MAX'S MUSICAL ABILITIES.

I WILL. SHE'S NOT GOOD.

BUT MAYBE THAT **TROLL** LIKED IT!

PEE-YOO!

HEY!

SPLOOSH!

NAB! GRAB!

HI, GUYS.

EGAD! AN OUTDOOR HOT TUB!

IT'S NOT A HOT TUB, KEVYN.

THEY'RE **COOKING** US!

AH. INDEED THEY ARE. THAT'S A WISE MOVE.

EATING US **RAW** MIGHT GIVE THEM **FOOD POISONING!**

"Let's talk about something else," Millie says, turning a bit green. "Getting eaten is one of my least favorite topics."

"Hang in there, we're not soup yet," I tell her. "You still have your wand, right?"

"I'd like to," she answers. "But my magic's not advanced enough to work on trolls."

"Perhaps it doesn't HAVE to be advanced!" cries Kevyn, his face brightening. "Remember what my book told us about these creatures?"

"It said they're slow-witted," Simon remembers.

"Precisely!" Kevyn exclaims. "These chaps are less brainy than a drawer full of socks!"

We scramble out of the cook pot and race away. The trolls don't notice a thing as we disappear into the foothills.

"BRILLIANT, Millie!" Kevyn cheers when we stop to rest. "Your magical improvisation was most effective!"

"I just wish I could do something for Sedgewick," she sighs.

"Then we'll need to find a piece of fruit—a REAL one," Kevyn states, unrolling our map.

We hike for a couple of hours, from the dusty hills of troll country and across a vast, grassy plain. "I think we're getting close," Simon notes. "I can smell the ocean!"

We continue to the outskirts of the town. It's smaller than Byjovia, but the streets are bustling with people. "Let's find the local market, shall we?" Kevyn urges.

"And priceless as that may be, it's no substitute for legal tender," Kevyn points out.

"Maybe we can TRADE something," Simon suggests.

"Or if worse comes to worst," Kevyn says . . .

6

"Great Scott!" Kevyn yelps. "Max, that's YOU!"

Simon squints at the poster. "No. The freckles and the ponytail are right, but the eyes are wrong."

Sorry, I guess "evil twin" might sound a little harsh. She's probably just hungry. But does she have to keep breaking the law? She's messing up BOTH our lives.

"Max, you must stay hidden!" Kevyn cautions. "If you're seen, you'll be arrested for your sister's crimes!"

There's a knot in my stomach as I watch Kevyn, Millie, and Simon walk away. I should be going with them. Instead, I'm hiding in this alley like a gutless wimp.

That reminds me—I need to disguise myself. I rummage through my bag until I find what I'm looking for.

Gadabout always says: "When in doubt, keep your mouth shut." So I stay quiet as this guy—whoever he is—swaggers toward me. As he closes in, I can smell salt water, seaweed . . .

Of COURSE I do. I'm a KNIGHT. But I have a feeling this clown's idea of adventure might be picking lice out of his beard. I give him my uncle Budrick-approved answer:

I whirl around, but it's too late. A couple of beefy guys throw a burlap sack over my head and sweep me into it.

I rack my brain for a way to escape. Can I CUT my way out of here? No, my dagger's buried in my backpack—which (duh) is on my back. And my arms are pinned to my sides.

It's a rough trip. These goons drop me a couple of times, and when I try to shout for help, the only answer I get is a swift kick in the ribs. A few bumpy minutes later, I'm dumped with a thud onto a hard wooden floor. I wriggle against the sack until . . .

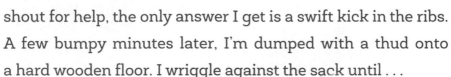

We climb aboard. The planks of the deck are battered and rotten. "If you're such an awesome buccaneer," I say ...

"That's why you grabbed me off the street?" I shout. "To be a CABIN BOY?"

"Aye," the pirate confirms. "You'll feed the crew, trim the sails, shiver the timbers ..."

That's it—I've heard enough. I slip my bag off my shoulders and reach for my blade. If these cutthroats mean to turn me into fish food . . .

"Well, I'm no pirate," I growl. "And I'm not going to be your cabin boy, either."

Cap'n Scab may have a salad fork for a hand, but his OTHER hand is pretty good at dueling. We go back and forth across the deck until . . .

Pretty dramatic, right? Maybe Kevyn would have said it better, but "blithering blowhard" isn't too shabby. The crew looks on, dumbstruck. The only sounds are the flapping of the sails and—

"Pull yourself together," I snap at him, "and take me back to dry land."

"I can't do that," Cap'n Scab replies.

I drop my dagger and rush to the railing. Sure enough, Peasoup is just a sliver on the horizon. Kevyn, Millie, and Simon are back there—with no idea what's happened to me.

"What I meant was, SOME pirates believe that a female on a ship brings bad luck!" Cap'n Scab explains. "But I think that's codswallop!"

Scab's grinning like he's just done me a favor, but I feel lower than a worm's belly. So what if I won our duel? It didn't change anything.

"Tremendous!" Cap'n Scab gushes. "Spectacular!"

Wait, MONTHS? Panic rises in my chest, but I force it back down. Steady, Max. Use your head.

"Uh . . . when you say 'supplies,'" I ask him . . .

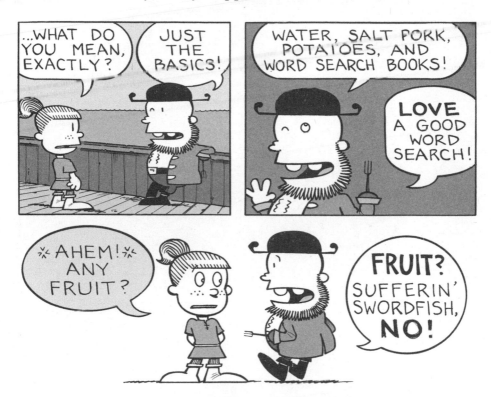

Nuts. There goes any chance I had of calling Mumblin.

"We sea rovers need HEARTY food," Scab continues.

Quick reminder: SEDGEWICK IS AN APPLE! He's in my backpack. And I left my backpack . . .

7

Excuse me for a sec while I save Sedgewick from this guy's digestive system.

The crewman's eyes narrow into slits. "A pet APPLE?" he scoffs. "That's weird, that is."

"Not really," another pirate chimes in.

Hold it. Who asked Droopy Drawers here for HIS opinion?
Now he's got the rest of the crew all hot and bothered.
They huddle around as he continues his rant.

"Why ELSE would she pretend to be a BOY?" he bellows.

SEA HAG?? Okay, that's just plain rude.

And THAT'S even RUDER. Wow, did this go sideways.
A minute ago, I was the plucky kid who beat Cap'n Scab.

"Steam my oysters," Scab curses. "You never told me what to call you, girl."

"I'm Max," I answer.

"MAX?" he echoes, shaking his head in confusion.

"Clam up, you jabbering jellyfish!" Scab thunders. "Max is no WITCH! She's just some gutter rat we snatched off the streets of Peasoup!"

"And what's that mean?" Cap'n Scab demands.

Droopy points a gnarled finger at me. "It means you have a choice: either SHE walks the plank . . ."

Yikes. Looks like I'm headed for that scenic tour of the ocean floor after all—unless I can talk my way out of this.

"Um ... hey, guys," I say. "Speaking of planks ..."

Hmm. Not a peep from the audience. I guess when Uncle Budrick says there's a joke for any occasion ...

Great. There's nothing I enjoy more than a leisurely stroll on a narrow piece of rotting wood. I tuck Sedgewick into my pocket. If I drown, he'll drown, too. But no worries.

I notice a wobble beneath my feet as I reach the end of the plank. It's springy, like a bowstring.

I grab the mast halfway up. From there I shimmy higher, all the way to the crow's nest. It's not exactly a real escape . . .

Two crewmen start scrambling up the pole, knives clenched in their teeth. I look around for anything I can use as a weapon. But the only thing I see is—

I'm not sure about that. From up here in the cheap seats, it looks like this so-called island is coming closer—but not because WE'RE moving.

"Holy haddock! You're right!"
Scab roars, peering through his
eyeglass. "It's Blotto!"

"Who's Blotto?" I call down.

WHEN SAILORS SPEAK OF MONSTERS VILE,
ONE CREATURE STANDS ALONE!
IT'S BLOTTO, FULL OF WRATH AND BILE,
WHO MAKES THEM QUAKE AND MOAN!

A MAMMOTH WHALE IN SEARCH OF PREY,
DESTRUCTION IS HIS KEN!
HE'S SUNK A HUNDRED SHIPS, THEY SAY,
AND KILLED TEN THOUSAND MEN!

Catchy tune. Too bad it doesn't come with instructions about what to do when Blotto attacks.

Ever been swallowed by a whale? It's actually not that bad. It doesn't hurt, and it's pretty dry in here, too. There's only one problem.

"Well, I follow a code, too—a KNIGHT'S code," I tell him. "That means it's my duty to get us out of this pickle."

"I'm all for it," Scab rasps. "But how?"

Good question. I look around for some answers. I'm no expert on whale guts, but we must be in Blotto's stomach—and we're definitely not the first thing he's eaten today.

The kiwi vibrates in my hand. Then—so faint I can barely hear it—comes the sound of Mumblin's voice.

"Max!" it hums. "Where on earth are you?"

"Fascinating," Mumblin observes. "What kind of fish?"

"A whale," I answer. That's when a second voice comes buzzing out of the kiwi.

I'm so happy to hear him, I don't even mind that he's being sort of a know-it-all.

Mumblin speaks again. "If you can get the whale to open its mouth, Max, I believe we can be of assistance."

"But we don't HAVE something pointy!" Grub blusters.

"Are you serious right now?" I ask.

SLOBBERIN' SEA BASS! A **DRAGON!**

THAT'S BRUCE! AND THE MIDKNIGHTS ARE WITH HIM!

SET US DOWN, GUYS!

Moments later, we're back on board the Scurvy Dog—but this time, I'm not staying long.

"Like what?"

"Anything at all!" he exclaims. "You never know when you might require the services of a dashing buccaneer!"

WHO'S STRONGER THAN A RISING TIDE?
WHO'S GREATER THAN THE OCEANS WIDE?
WHO SAVED OUR CLUELESS CAPTAIN'S HIDE?
IT'S MIGHTY, MIGHTY **MAX**!

MORE DARING THAN THE BRAVEST LAD!
AND FEARSOME WHEN YOU MAKE HER MAD!
BEST CABIN BOY WE'VE EVER HAD!
SHE'S MIGHTY, MIGHTY **MAX**!

8

"Don't let it go to your head, Max," Simon jokes after I've joined the rest of the Midknights on Bruce's back.

"What do you mean?"

"The SONG!" he whoops.

"Long story," I answer. "How'd you guys find me?"

"Sheer dumb luck!" Mumblin giggles. "When your friends contacted me . . ."

"But there were no visible landmarks that revealed where the ship WAS!" explains Kevyn.

"Only miles and miles of ocean," Millie adds.

"That's when I summoned Bruce to help us search for you," continues Mumblin.

"Landed WHERE?" I holler into the wind as we soar above the mammoth ocean. "All I see is WATER!"

"A temporary situation," Mumblin assures me. "At this speed, we'll reach the Faithless Forest within the hour."

Oh, yeah—HER. Thanks to my unplanned vacation on the *Scurvy Dog*, I'd almost forgotten about looking for Mary. I try to imagine meeting her again. I mean, what'll I SAY?

Hmmm. Can't think of a decent opening line. Maybe I'll just kick her in the shins. Anyway, Bruce is circling down toward a clearing. Looks like we're here.

Mumblin sighs. "I'm old—that's what's wrong. My knees are shot, my nose hair is out of control, and my magical powers have all the potency of weak tea."

"Or to put it more colorfully . . ." Kevyn chirps.

"Are you okay, Sedgewick?" Millie asks.

"Yeah, I think so," he confirms, looking a little dazed. "Thanks for bringing me back. It was getting pretty crowded inside Max's pocket."

I WAS SHARING THE SPACE WITH TWO PEBBLES, A SEASHELL, THREE PIECES OF BUBBLE GUM, A LUTE STRING, A TOOTH, A DEAD LADYBUG, AND TWELVE BUTTONS.

HEH HEH! WHAT A PACK RAT!

I LIKE TO COLLECT STUFF! SO SUE ME!

THANKS FOR THE LIFT, BRUCE! WE'LL TRAVEL ON FOOT FROM HERE!

The dragon flies off, and we follow Mumblin along a narrow path that traces the edge of the forest. "Where are we going?" Simon wonders.

"To visit a friend who can help us," Mumblin explains.

"A friend?" I repeat.

... OR A **GIRLFRIEND**? NYUK NYUK!

✳AHEM!✳ WELL...

MUMBLEKINS!

"MUMBLEKINS"?

PUMPKIN HEAD!

"I fail to comprehend why pumpkin head is a term of endearment," Kevyn declares. I don't get it, either, but it's working for Mumblin. There's a whole lot of endearment going on over there.

"Really?" I say, relieved to stop talking about snogging with Sedgewick. "You know where she is?"

Beatrice shakes her head. "Not at this moment. But she and her guardian always return to these woods. I can take you to where I last saw them."

"I don't think they live ANYWHERE," Beatrice replies. "They're constantly on the move, you see."

"There's more to it than that," Beatrice advises. "It's widely believed that King Rotgut of Klunk wants the girl dead."

"DEAD?" Millie cries. "But WHY?"

"I don't know," Beatrice admits. "But there are rumors that she has royal blood—that she is a relative of the king!"

"Wait," I break in. "If MARY'S somehow related to Rotgut..."

"Let's not get ahead of ourselves," Mumblin cautions.
"Before we react to something, let's make certain it's REAL."

Appearing from out of the forest—it still feels freaky to say this—is my twin sister. And I'm not really getting a warm and fuzzy family vibe.

"You don't need that blade, Mary," I tell her.

Not THIS again. First the pirates, now her. How come everyone's trying so hard to make me a sorceress?

Mumblin speaks up. "If you'll allow me, I shall reveal why Max knows your name."

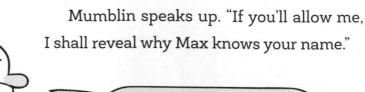

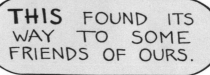

"That's my locket!" Mary's guardian cries, her eyes flashing.

"I'd be happy to return it to you," Mumblin offers.

"Why?" snaps the woman. "Is there a HEX on it?"

"Of course not," Mumblin responds. "No self-respecting wizard would resort to such tactics."

Mary whirls toward her companion. "Ah-HA! Did you hear that, Perrin?"

Deep breaths, Max. Just because she's your sister doesn't mean she isn't a complete moron.

"Listen," I say through gritted teeth. "I am not a witch."

"Then why do you look just like me?" Mary demands.

Her face turns whiter than a pail of milk. She knows it's true—I can tell. But she's not willing to buy in just yet.

"I don't have a twin," she protests.

"There can be no doubt, I think, that Max and Mary are sisters," Mumblin says. "What we're trying to learn is—"

"You're called MAX?" Mary interrupts loudly.

"Why don't we all sit down and talk ... as friends?" Beatrice suggests. "Perhaps we'll find some answers!"

I start a fire the old fashioned way Mary and Perrin probably aren't ready for one of Millie's meat loaf specials. We form a circle and Mumblin begins, explaining how Uncle Budrick found me, that I know nothing about my parents . . .

"Did you find Mary in a church doorway, too?" I ask.

Perrin shakes her head. "No, she was given to me. But the story begins before that."

"Ah, jolly good!" Kevyn exults. "A tale by firelight!"

"Hey!" I break in. "He's the hunky guy Conrad picked to marry King Rotgut's daughter—the princess!"

"Emeline," Perrin affirms. "Yes, that's right."

"Uh . . . what does 'eloped' mean?" Simon wonders.

"They snuck away to be married in private," Kevyn offers.

Sedgewick frowns. "But I thought the whole point was to unite the kingdoms—you know, make it official."

Perrin nods and continues her story. "A year went by. Most assumed that Reginald and Emeline were gone forever."

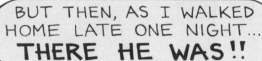

"Sir Reginald?" we all ask.

"No," Perrin answers.

IT WAS A **BABY**!

KEEP THIS CHILD HIDDEN! PLEASE! FOR THE SAKE OF THE **PRINCESS**!

!

SHE MUST NOT BE FOUND — ESPECIALLY BY THE **KING**!

HER LIFE IS AT STAKE! DO YOU UNDERSTAND?

Y-YES.

THEN GO! **RUN**!

AS I DASHED OFF, I HEARD THE SOUND OF BOOTS APPROACHING...

AND FROM THE SHADOWS, I SAW THE SQUIRE CAPTURED BY KING ROTGUT'S SOLDIERS.

"That's how I became Mary's guardian," Perrin concludes. "And it's why we live as we do—running and hiding to avoid being found by the king's men."

My head is spinning. Beside me, Mumblin takes a deep breath. "My goodness," he says.

"Well, won't Reginald and Emeline have all the answers?" Simon points out. "Let's go looking for THEM!"

"We can't," Mary says softly.

"Great Scott!" Kevyn whispers. "How dastardly!"

"This is why I asked you to send me into the past," I remind Mumblin. "So that instead of depending on memories . . ."

"It's not possible," Mumblin counters. "As I've already told Max, there is no way to magically revisit the past."

After a long pause, Beatrice breaks the silence. "That's not entirely true, Snuggle Butt."

"It's not a spell, a potion, or an enchantment," Beatrice says. "But there's a PLACE deep in the Faithless Forest where it is said one can travel into yesteryear."

"The Tower of Time!" Kevyn repeats, his face bright with excitement. "I say! ..."

THAT WOULD BE A SMASHING **BOOK TITLE!**

YOU SAID THE SAME THING ABOUT "KEVYN'S FIELD GUIDE TO EXOTIC GOURDS AND SQUASHES."

"Er . . . yes, well, perhaps that wasn't one of my more scintillating efforts," he admits.

"I would, if I knew where it is," says Honey Lips—I mean, Beatrice. "Its location is a secret."

"How can that be?" Millie wonders. "If it really does offer the chance to visit the past . . ."

"That's US!" I exclaim. "If we don't find the tower . . ."

"By who?" I ask.

"Whom," Kevyn corrects me. Because grammar is so important in moments like this.

"I don't hear anything," Simon whispers.

These must be King Rotgut's men. They're on us quickly, but Perrin's warning gained us a few precious seconds. Mumblin, Beatrice, and Millie all have their wands out.

ZAP!

POFF!

CROAK.

REALLY? **FROGS**? THAT'S SO **CHEESEBALL**!

ACTUALLY, I THINK THOSE ARE TOADS.

DON'T PICK 'EM UP, SIMON! THEY'LL GIVE YOU WARTS!

OR PEE IN YOUR HAND!

HOW APPALLINGLY UNSANITARY.

THEY WON'T BE TOADS FOR LONG.

INDEED. THEY'LL TURN BACK INTO MEN IN A MATTER OF MINUTES.

SNORT!

!

GUYS, **LOOK**!

"Correction—they belong to US now!" Kevyn declares with a wave of his finger. "According to Byjovia's constitution, possession is nine-tenths of the law!"

"I didn't know Byjovia HAD a constitution," I say.

"I wrote it last week," Kevyn explains. "I needed a project."

Mary's eyes flash. "Of course, I do," she thunders. "While YOU'VE been living the posh life in Byjovia, I'VE been learning survival skills in the wild!"

"I'm not posh," I sputter, heat rising in my cheeks.

"I suggest you set aside this argument, ladies," Mumblin breaks in. "You have to get started."

"Uh . . . don't you mean WE?" I ask him. "You're coming with us, right, Mumblin?"

He shakes his head. "I'll leave the journeying to you and the other Midknights, Max."

"Nothing quite so haunting," Perrin says kindly.

"Then you mustn't delay," Beatrice states.

"One last thing," Mumblin says. From his robes, he takes the locket that started this whole adventure and hands it to Perrin. "This belongs to you."

Perrin leads the way on foot. The rest of us double up on horseback. I'm with Simon, Kevyn's with Millie, and—I feel a twinge of annoyance in my gut—Mary rides with Sedgewick.

"Traveling by night isn't ideal," Perrin apologizes, "but we need to put some distance between us and those soldiers." And with that, we plunge into the Faithless Forest to begin our search for the Tower of Time.

"It's weird that something as big as a tower could stay hidden," Simon says as we make our way among the trees.

"It's probably magically concealed," Millie suggests.

...SORT OF LIKE BENTLEY'S PASS!

UGH. HOPE WE NEVER SEE **THAT** PLACE AGAIN!

YOU'VE BEEN TO BENTLEY'S PASS?

HAVE WE **EVER**! JUST ASK SEDGEWICK!

HE GOT TURNED INTO AN **APPLE**!

✳ CHUCKLE! ✳ YES, IT'S A RATHER "SEEDY" STORY!

I'VE HEARD THAT BENTLEY'S PASS IS SUPER **DANGEROUS**!

"Oh, we've been to places way more dangerous than that," Simon insists, sounding impressively casual.

"Luckily, Bruce rescued us," I add.

Mary scowls. "You must take me for a fool. I know tall tales when I hear them."

I glare right back at her. "They're not tall tales."

"Well, you're doing a pretty fair job of it," she snaps.

  ...SO I GUESS YOU'RE **NOT A KNIGHT AFTER ALL!**

That stings. I'm so mad, I can barely see. I'd like to shove a knuckle sandwich right in Mary's ugly face.

But wait. We're TWINS. If I call HER ugly . . .

...AM I CALLING **MYSELF** UGLY?

OH, MAX IS A KNIGHT, ALL RIGHT!

YOU SHOULD SEE HER HANDLE A BOW AND ARROW!

Wow, nice shout-out from Sedgewick! For an instant, I have a wild urge to hug him. I might even try it, too . . .

...IF **MARY** WEREN'T **HANGING ALL OVER HIM!**

PSST... YOU OKAY?

"What do you mean?" I ask. (News flash: I'm pretty sure I know what he means.)

Simon slows our pace, and we fall behind the others.

WELL... SEEMS LIKE YOU DON'T REALLY ENJOY HAVING A SISTER.

"Not A sister," I grumble. "Just THIS sister. She's totally obnoxious!"

DID YOU HEAR HER CALL ME A **LIAR?**

"That wasn't great," Simon concedes. "But try to look at it from HER side."

"What do you mean?"

"She's lived her whole life on the run! That means she doesn't know how to trust people!"

...INCLUDING **YOU.**

SO HOW DO I GET HER TO TRUST ME?

I DON'T KNOW.

Perrin's kneeling up ahead, gazing intently at something on the ground. The rest of us dismount and join her.

A grimy and thickset figure lumbers out of the brush, blocking the path before us. In one of his meaty fists he clutches a soldier's broadsword. But this is no soldier.

"What do you want with us?" Perrin demands.

The stranger pulls a rumpled sheet of parchment from his tunic. I recognize it right away—it's the picture of Mary from the poster we saw in Peasoup.

"THIS is the prize I seek!" he bellows.

Perrin growls back at him. "You're a bounty hunter."

A wicked grin creases his face. "That's right."

Perrin reaches for her dagger, but the stranger is too quick for her. With one violent swipe of  his arm, he knocks her to the ground. She falls against a tree stump and lies still. She's out cold.

The stranger roars with rage. "Oh, yes, she IS, you mouthy little whelp—straight to Rotgut's dungeon!"

Whew. That was close. To my left, I see Millie pull out her wand. Maybe she can turn this bruiser into a walnut or something. But when she motions at him, nothing happens.

As we duel, I can tell the stranger isn't used to fighting against someone so small. That gives me an edge. I can duck underneath his sword . . .

I've never stabbed a bad guy before—but this dude smells so horrible, let's consider it a public service. The sword tumbles out of his hand. Before he can recover, I grab it.

I pick up the scrap of parchment with Mary's picture on it. The stranger watches as I crumple it into a ball.

"You'll collect no bounty on her," I tell him.

He gives me a murderous look. "What are you?" he barks. "Her bodyguard?"

I shake my head. "No."

Simon and I both have some rope in our backpacks, and we use it to tie up our furry friend. He's probably strong enough to work his way loose in a few hours...

"You shouldn't walk, then," I remind her as we get ready to resume our journey.

"That's a grand idea," Perrin says, and closes her eyes. I've always heard that experienced riders can sleep on horseback, but until now I've never seen it . . .

Ha! Uncle Budrick's the same way. I'm all set to tell Mary about the time his snoring shattered a window—TWO BLOCKS AWAY—but she's got something else on her mind.

"I . . . um . . . just wanted to say . . ." she begins.

THANKS FOR STICKING UP FOR ME WITH THAT BOUNTY HUNTER.

I shrug. "No problem. He didn't look like the type to talk it out over tea and biscuits, so . . ."

"So you DUELED him!"

I CAN'T BELIEVE YOU TOOK HIM ON! HE WAS **HUGE!**

I start to say that it was no big deal, that I've fought against gargoyles and bodkins and any other baddie you could dream up. But then I remember what Simon said:

TRY TO LOOK AT IT FROM **MARY'S** SIDE!

Hmm. Maybe I'll just keep my mouth shut.

Wow, look who's being Miss Friendly all of a sudden. Having a sister might be less horrible than I thought.

"That's okay," I say. "I'm actually not a full-fledged knight yet. I'm still in school."

Mary sighs. "I wish I could go to school."

"It's not all it's cracked up to be," I assure her.

 I HAVE NO HOME.

She doesn't say it like she wants me to feel sorry for her. But I do.

And there's some guilt mixed in there, too. I've got a house . . . my own room . . . a bed. What does Mary have?

We've come to a clearing next to a small pond. Simon waters the horses while the rest of us prepare to bed down.

"I don't understand," Millie moans. "This wand is brand new! Why isn't it working?"

"The wand isn't the problem," Perrin explains. "These woods have their own brand of witchcraft. The deeper into the Faithless Forest we travel..."

IN OTHER WORDS, YOU HAVEN'T CHANGED A BIT!

OH, **HO!** TOUCHÉ!

SKRITCH SKRITCH

"Well, I can guarantee there won't be any tuna in this pond." Simon chuckles, pulling some fishing line from his pocket.

BUT MAYBE I CAN CATCH SOME **TROUT** FOR SUPPER!

GURGLE

HISSSSSSSS

"Um . . . that's not a trout," Sedgewick says.

"An unarguable observation," Kevyn agrees.

Okay, then, what IS this thing? It's more than just a column of water. It's making noise. It has a face.

Mary plants her feet at the edge of the pond and stares straight at the creature. I can't help but feel a rush of admiration. That's pretty gutsy.

A slow hiss escapes its mouth. Then, deep and wet like the roar of a waterfall, comes a voice.

"I am the guardian of the Tower of Time," it says.

"YES, I'm a girl!" the creature rumbles, sounding annoyed. "Why does everyone assume I'm a BOY?"

"Nearer than you know," answers the guardian. "I will gladly reveal its whereabouts. All you must do in exchange is solve this simple riddle."

YOU CANNOT BUILD ME, CANNOT BAKE ME, CANNOT THROW OR KICK OR SHAKE ME. LISTEN WELL, FOR ONCE YOU MAKE ME, YOU AND YOU ALONE CAN BREAK ME.

WHAT AM I?

Perrin grimaces. "That's a puzzler, all right."

"How many guesses do we get?" Mary asks.

Kathy's hollow eyes narrow into a scowl. "One."

"If we put our heads together, we'll solve this," Sedgewick says. "But we've only got one shot. Let's all pledge not to shout out an answer before we've agreed on it."

"Okay, Kathy," I shout. "Bring us to the Tower of Time!"

"No," the guardian howls, sinking back into the water. "I will bring the Tower to YOU."

The surface of the pond begins to ripple and froth. We feel the ground tremble beneath our feet. Then . . .

"The Tower of Time, I presume," purrs Kevyn as the rest of us stare up in amazement.

"It's either that or a giant wedding cake," Simon cracks.

"No wonder it's so hard to find this thing," Sedgewick notes. "It's hidden in the pond!"

WELL, WE'D BETTER GET INSIDE BEFORE IT **SINKS** AGAIN!

We approach the entrance. I pull on the handle, but it doesn't budge. "The door's locked," I announce.

PERHAPS THE CORRECT SEQUENCE OF **WORDS** WILL ALLOW US TO GAIN ADMITTANCE!

GOOD IDEA!

YO! LET US IN!

BAM! BAM!

I IMAGINED SOMETHING A BIT MORE POETIC, BUT WHATEVS.

KLICK!

HEY! IT **WORKED!**

SOMEBODY'S OPENING THE DOOR!

WITCH EVRA?!

"Why are you here instead of at Bentley's Pass?" I ask.

She shrugs. "I was transferred. It was a lateral move."

"We've come to climb the Tower of Time," I tell her, "and travel back into yesteryear."

"ALL of you?" Evra clucks. "Oh, no, no, no. I'm afraid not."

"Sorry, dearies, but I've got to follow the rules," the little witch maintains. "Otherwise, I'll be demoted!"

IT'LL BE GOODBYE, TOWER OF TIME... HELLO, TOWER OF **SLIME!**

...WHICH, NEEDLESS TO SAY, ISN'T THE MOST POPULAR TOURIST DESTINATION.

GUYS! HUDDLE UP!

We retreat to a nearby grove of trees where Witch Evra can't eavesdrop. "There must be a way to smuggle me and Mary in there together!" I whisper.

"Millie, can you make one of them invisible?" Simon asks.

She flicks her wand a bunch of times with no results. "Sorry," she groans. "My magic is completely shut down."

WHAT WOULD **MUMBLIN** DO IN A SPOT LIKE THIS?

MAYBE HE'S DONE SOMETHING **ALREADY!**

"Perrin," I say excitedly, "where's the locket?"

"Right here," she answers, pulling it from her bag and handing it to me. "But how will the locket help?"

"What did Mumblin say when he returned this to you?"

I flip open the locket. I was right—it begins to vibrate in my hand. The picture of Mary tucked inside dissolves into tiny pinpoints of light. Then, like a cloud of fireflies, they flitter out of the metal casing, and . . .

Mary's surrounded by the cloud. Then, all at once, she BECOMES the cloud, which stretches into a glowing ribbon leading back toward me. It coils into the locket, which snaps shut on its own.

"Open it, Max," Millie whispers. I pry the two halves apart, and we all peer inside.

Perrin is flabbergasted. "That's a different picture of Mary than was there before!"

"A few minutes are all we'll need," I say. I tuck the locket inside my tunic and walk over to the base of the Tower.

"I'm ready," I say to Witch Evra.

She side-eyes me. "Why you and not your sister?"

"Yes," Kevyn concedes. "But I'm not a person."

"Good luck, Max!" Millie calls as we follow Witch Evra through the entryway. "Be careful!"

"And take care of M—of yourself," Perrin adds.

I nod, feeling the locket against my skin. "Count on it."

Evra leads us into a mammoth chamber. It's empty. I point to a steep flight of stairs hugging the wall.

"So . . . uh . . . should we start climbing?"

NOW she tells us. And without another word, Witch Evra disappears in a puff of smoke, leaving us standing there with no map, no instructions—NOTHING.

Kevyn's ready to cough up a hair ball. "How distressing," he gripes. "Who's going to lead us into the past?"

"NO!"

That's the only thing I can think to say. Truthfully, it's all I feel CAPABLE of saying. Because this absolutely, positively cannot be happening.

"THIS IS IMPOSSIBLE!" I shout. "Why are YOU here?"

The onetime king—FAKE king—of Byjovia smirks. "Why SHOULDN'T I be here?"

"Because you got carried off by a . . . a herd . . . a flock . . . er . . ."

"In other words, you CHEATED!" Gastley sneers.

"I'm ready to get started," she replies, and hooks a thumb in Gastley's direction. "Who's the dude with the weak mustache?"

He glares at her. "What a charming child," he mutters, sounding totally uncharmed. "Before we begin, I must first list the three most important rules of time travel."

1. STAY HIDDEN, 2. INTERACT WITH NO ONE, AND 3. DO NOTHING THAT COULD POTENTIALLY CHANGE THE FUTURE!

"What?" Mary wails. "So if we find our parents, we're not allowed to TALK to them?"

"Those are the rules, you little brat," snaps Gastley.

ER... I MEAN, YOU'RE ENTIRELY CORRECT, MY DEAR!

PAT PAT

Ugh. I don't trust Gastley as far as I can throw him, but we need a guide. "Okay, we won't break any rules," I say.

LEAD THE WAY.

I'D BE HAPPY TO!

I'VE ALWAYS BEEN A NATURAL-BORN LEADER!

RIIIIIIIIIGHT.

We follow Gastley up the winding staircase. Every few steps we pass by a door, each identical to the last. Finally, he stops at one and twists the handle. It swings open.

"This doorway is the first leg of your journey," he announces. "You will be observing events from approximately eleven years ago. Oh, and just a reminder . . ."

IT'S . . . ✳AHEM!✳ . . . CUSTOMARY TO **TIP** YOUR GUIDE!

YOU WANT A TIP, DUDE?

TRY A BREATH MINT!

OOH! ✳CHORTLE!✳ **BURN!**

WELL, HERE GOES NOTHING!

We leave Gastley on the stairs and cross the threshold into a large room. Columns line the walls, and velvet curtains hang from the ceiling. On a marble platform at the far end of the chamber rests a single piece of furniture: a throne.

We duck behind a curtain only seconds before King Rotgut stalks into the room, barking orders at a black-robed character scurrying after him.

"Our spies estimate that Byjovia's army numbers fifty thousand," the one called Trotwell reports.

Rotgut leans back on his throne and grimaces. "Bah. We can't hope to defeat so strong an opponent," he growls.

THAT'S WHY MY **PLAN** IS SO... SO... UHH...

GIVE ME A WORD, TROTWELL.

"BRILLIANT," YOUR HIGHNESS.

"Yes!" Rotgut agrees. "My plan is brilliant! Its brilliance is absolutely . . . um . . . hmm . . ."

GIVE ME ANOTHER WORD, TROTWELL.

DING-A-LING!

DID YOU JUST CALL ME A DING-A-LING?

N-**NO**, YOUR KINGSHIP! IT WAS YOUR **PAGE BOY**!

WHAT IS IT, PAGE BOY?

YOUR MAJESTY, ANNOUNCING PRINCESS EMELINE AND SIR REGINALD!

A thrill shoots up my spine, and I hear Mary gasp as she grabs my arm. We're both thinking the same thing:

"Emeline! Reginald!" Rotgut cries, a forced cheerfulness suddenly infecting his voice.

My heart is pounding as I hear Emeline's—MY MOTHER'S—voice for the first time. There's a lump the size of a magic grapefruit in my throat. I sneak a glance at Mary. She wipes something from her cheek.

"Ah! Boating!" booms Rotgut.

The king scowls. "Who the devil is Clayton?"

"I am, Your Highness," Reginald's squire replies.

"Fine, your service is noted," Rotgut grunts impatiently.

"But take your leave, all of you. I must speak to Reginald . . ."

The others exit the throne room. Once they're gone, the king leans close to Reginald.

"Give me your update, you useless lump," he orders. "When you're not busy getting bested by your SQUIRE . . ."

Rotgut snickers. "Ha! Conrad! That bumbling fool has no idea you work for ME! But we must act before he suspects! The sooner you marry Princess Emeline . . ."

We listen in horror as the two men burst into wicked laughter. "This is terrible!" I whisper. "Rotgut's using this arranged marriage as a way to destroy Byjovia!"

"And you know what makes it worse?" Mary murmurs.

Behind us, Gastley stands in the frame of the doorway leading back to the Tower. "Remember the rules!" he cautions. "You can't intervene in events from the past! And besides, there's much more for you to see. Come this way!"

"Of course," he boasts. "I've spent YEARS studying every nook and cranny of this Tower!"

"YEARS?" I repeat. "Who are you kidding?"

YOU ONLY DISAPPEARED FROM BYJOVIA A FEW **MONTHS** AGO!

"Inside the Tower of Time, a CENTURY can pass in a heartbeat!" he says. "But I don't expect YOU to understand that!"

YOU'RE **CHILDREN!**

TECHNICALLY, I'M A FELINE.

SO YOU'VE OPENED EVERY DOOR IN THIS JOINT, HUH?

ENOUGH QUESTIONS!

WE'VE ARRIVED AT THE NEXT LEG OF YOUR JOURNEY.

ENTER. A FEW WEEKS HAVE PASSED SINCE YOUR PREVIOUS TIME JUMP.

I FEEL OLDER ALREADY.

AT LEAST YOU'RE NOT AGING IN **CAT YEARS.**

Kevyn, Mary, and I step through the doorway, but we're not in the throne room this time.

We move toward the
sound, staying hidden
behind a line of shrubs.

Our mother speaks softly, but her answer is firm. "No, Reginald. I've made myself very clear."

Even from a distance, I can see the shock on Reginald's face. "What foolishness is this, squire?" he bellows. "The princess is no concern of yours!"

"But she is," Clayton counters. "I love her."

There's a glint of steel as Reginald draws his sword.

It's not a fair contest. Clayton's a good fighter, but the size of Reginald's weapon is too much for him.

Clayton takes the sword from Reginald, who stares in amazement at Emeline.

"What kind of princess carries a dagger?" he whines.

"I doubt that," Clayton says. "How will he react when you admit that you lost the princess to a lowly squire?"

"And I'll make certain that everyone in Byjovia learns of your vile treachery," Clayton adds. "So I wouldn't go back there if I were you."

Reginald stalks away to the north. From our hiding place, we watch Clayton and Emeline branch off to the east.

There's a long silence. Finally, Mary turns to me, her eyes blazing with excitement. "Max," she whispers. "Do you realize what this MEANS?"

She looks baffled. "What's a 'high five'?"

"Simon and I invented it," I say. "It's something friends do when they're happy."

"Ohhhh," she says "Oh, I know what that is. But where
I come from . . ."

"Hurry up, you miserable worms!" Gastley shouts when we arrive back at the doorway.

"If you're in a rush," Mary tells him, "you could have just come and found us."

"Honor?" I complain to Kevyn as we continue our climb up the Tower steps.

Mary turns pale. "Ew. You eat RATS?"

"Perhaps not rats," Kevyn admits.

The stairs have grown steadily steeper and narrower. You can't even call them steps anymore.

"Several months have passed since last time," Gastley says, pushing open a creaking door. "Proceed with caution."

We enter a musty room. Stacks of books reach the ceiling, and against the far wall there's an assortment of jars and vials.

"This is a sorcerer's lair," Kevyn whispers.

Okay, no idea what a "lair" is. But I recognize the sorcerer. It's Trotwell. We scoot behind some boxes in the corner, only seconds before King Rotgut comes barreling through the door.

"Princess Emeline and Sir Reginald eloped nearly a YEAR ago!" he rages, spit flying from his mouth.

Nothing like a death threat to provide some instant motivation. Trotwell rushes to a nearby closet and rummages through the clutter.

Sounds like this magic melon is Trotwell's version of Mumblin's grapefruit. We watch as the old man taps the melon with his wand. He taps it again. And again.

"Aha! So I'm going to be a grandfather!" Rotgut crows, making it all about him. "Now I see why she's been in hiding!"

I give Mary a wink. What would ol' Rotbutt say if he knew those twins were so close by, we could count his cavities?

"Brilliant!" the king exults. "Two BOYS, no doubt! They shall become the strapping young princes of Klunk!"

"Er . . . they won't belong only to Klunk, sire," Trotwell points out. "Their father is from Byjovia."

Rotqut sneers, "You nattering nitwit! Do you honestly think I'd allow my daughter to marry a BYJOVIAN?"

Trotwell is still gazing at the melon. "If I may say so . . ."

From our hiding spot, Mary and I watch our parents embrace. It's totally romantic. Right, Rotgut?

Rotgut turns the color of a ripe plum. I sense a tantrum coming on. Cover your ears, everybody.

The king rants and raves for a good two minutes. Then, finally spent, he sinks into a chair.

"No grandsons of mine will have Byjovian blood," he vows.

I'm expecting Tirade Part II, but Rotgut holds it together. "We'll find them," he grumbles. "Trotwell, tell our soldiers to search every building within one hundred miles."

Mary can't help herself. She gasps—and it's not one of those prissy gasps, either. She lets it rip.

"What was that?" Rotgut grunts, rising from his chair.

Kevyn struts out into the open and straight up to Rotgut. What is he DOING??

AHEM! MEOW.

AH. **THAT** MUST BE WHAT YOU HEARD, YOUR MAJESTY.

THERE ARE STRAY CATS THROUGHOUT THE CASTLE.

AND ARE THEY ALL AS UGLY AS **THIS** ONE?

FSSSST!

BOOT!

SCRAM, FLEABAG!

Rotgut turns on his heel and stalks out of the room. "Come, Trotwell," he barks. "We'll muster the soldiers." Mary and I rush over to Kevyn.

SO MUCH FOR MY CAT-LIKE REFLEXES.

GREAT JOB, KEVYN!

YOU KEPT ROTGUT FROM SNIFFING OUT OUR HIDING SPOT!

"That's where our guide comes in," I say as we dash for the doorway. We leap through the opening and find ourselves back in the Tower. And guess what? There's nobody here.

"We've got no choice," I answer. "We push on."

Higher and higher we climb along the winding stairway. We're talking NOSEBLEED territory. We force open every door we see—the right one's got to be here somewhere— but none of them takes us where we need to go.

ZAP!

A bolt of excitement shoots through me. "It's TROTWELL!"
I say, "This must be the right timeline after all!"

We pad along silently, keeping Trotwell in sight through a maze of moonlit alleys.

"Do you think he's on his way to . . . kill our mom and dad?" Mary whispers. She can barely get the words out.

"No," Kevyn states. "First, he has no soldiers with him."

AND SECOND, HE DOESN'T SEEM LIKE A MURDEROUS KIND OF CHAP!

WELL, WHATEVER HE'S PLANNING, I GUESS IT'S HAPPENING IN THAT SHACK.

SHOULD WE GO IN AFTER HIM?

WE **CAN'T!** REMEMBER THE RULES OF TIME TRAVEL?

YEAH, BUT THOSE WERE **GASTLEY'S** RULES!

SHHH! LISTEN!

There are voices coming from inside. We tiptoe across the cobblestones and then edge along the wall to an open window.

"Mortal danger?" Clayton echoes. "How can that be? They were born only a few hours ago!"

"We've not even given them NAMES yet!" Emeline adds.

"That means nothing to your father," Trotwell continues. "He has commanded that they be . . . dealt with."

Our two-timing Tower guide swoops into the room and plucks the babies from their cradles. This won't end well. Not unless we do something about it.

Gastley smirks. "Let's just say Rotgut isn't the ONLY king who wants these infants . . . out of the way."

"You're no king," I snarl.

"Not anymore," he hisses. "Thanks to YOU."

"What about your so-called Pledge of Honor?" I shout. "You shouldn't even BE here!"

"Nor should YOU," he replies with an evil grin.

A bite on the ankle may not be the knightliest move, but it gets the job done. Mary and I are there to catch the babies. Clayton grabs Gastley's broadsword.

Emeline rushes toward us. "My precious girls!"

Clayton runs to the window. "It's true! There's a patrol coming this way!"

He darts outside. Seconds later, we hear shouts and the clashing of metal. Sounds like Clayton has his hands full.

The princess seizes Trotwell by the arm. "What can we do to protect my children?"

"They must be hidden, my lady . . ."

"That's the problem," Trotwell explains. "I quite foolishly revealed that very fact to your father."

Clayton staggers back inside, bruised and bleeding. "I was able to drive them away," he announces.

Mary gazes at the baby in her arms. "Max," she whispers.

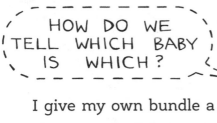

I give my own bundle a quick once-over. "This one's me," I say. "I recognize the birthmark behind her ear."

I fold the card twice and tuck it into the baby's tiny fist. "Hold on to this, little gal," I murmur.

"Excuse me," our mother says, gazing intently at Mary and me.

"I don't mean to be rude . . ."

I'm dying to tell her. We BOTH are. But what if saying something messes up the future? We can't risk it.

"We're ... uh ... just a couple of strangers," I answer.

I hand myself to Trotwell—there's a bizarre phrase—and Mary gives her mini-me to Clayton. He looks worried.

"The streets will be crawling with your father's men," he says to Emeline.

This is a funky thing to say in a situation like ours, but time stands still for a moment. Then Clayton eases the door open to make sure it's safe outside. A second later, he and Trotwell sneak silently away from the shack.

Our mom turns to me and Mary. "You two should go as well," she tells us. "When the soldiers arrive, this will be no place for children."

Gastley's still on the floor. I pull out Perrin's locket and flip it open. With any luck, there's a bit of magic left in it.

"Wow, what a wuss," Mary scoffs as she watches Gastley turn into a junior fireworks display and get sucked into the locket. "When that happened to ME . . ."

I feel Emeline's hand pushing hard against my shoulder. I stumble through the doorway, expecting to find myself in some sort of hidden alley. But that's not where we end up.

"That's impossible!" I protest. "We went into the past! We spent hours climbing stairs!"

"Yes, but remember what Gastley said about time behaving differently inside the Tower," Kevyn reminds me.

"Whoa, whoa," Simon chimes in.

"What went on in there, Max?" Millie asks. "Did you see Emeline and Reginald?"

I nod. "Uh-huh. And Clayton."

UM...TIME OUT. WHO'S **CLAYTON**?

THAT'S WHAT **WE** WANTED TO KNOW.

And with that, I tell them about everything—Rotgut's evil plan, Reginald being a scumbag, and the discovery that Clayton is our real dad.

"What a story!" Millie says when I've finished. "I'm almost afraid to ask, but . . . are your parents still alive?"

"We don't know," Mary replies. "We got pulled out of the past before we could see what happened next."

BUT THEY WERE ALIVE WHEN **WE** SAW THEM!

AND THEY **STILL** ARE! I CAN **FEEL** IT!

"Jolly good! Let's think positively!" Kevyn cheers. "If their lives were spared..."

...WHERE WOULD ROTGUT HIDE THEM, PERRIN?

HMM...

IN HIS DEADLIEST PRISON: THE **BRIMSTONE QUARRY!**

Mary looks stricken. "They say prisoners are worked to DEATH in that place!" she cries.

"That's the rumor," Perrin concedes. "But nobody knows for certain."

We mount up, and Perrin leads us on a twisting route through the Faithless Forest. Every few hours, we stop to rest and water the horses.

During one of our breaks, Mary looks troubled. "Max," she says, "why didn't she come with us?"

"Who?"

Jinx—we both have the same question. And with any luck, we'll get an answer soon. We climb back on the horses and keep riding, all through the night and the next day.

We look down on a brutal scene. Ragged figures in chains swing picks while armed guards look on. I guess the rumors about this place are true: these poor people look half-dead already. But here's the upside:

KLUNKHOUNDS ARE VICIOUS! WE'LL NEVER GET PAST THEM!

YES, WE WILL! WE JUST NEED A DIVERSION!

KEVYN! TIME TO **ROCK** 'N' ROLL!

GET IT? ROCK? QUARRY?

WAIT, ARE YOU ASKING ME TO BE **BAIT**?

JUST DISTRACT THE DOGS LONG ENOUGH FOR US TO SNEAK INSIDE!

"DISTRACT" THEM? THEY'LL MAKE ME THEIR **CHEW TOY**!

I FERVENTLY HOPE THAT CATS REALLY **DO** HAVE NINE LIVES!

The rest of us wait behind a boulder. "As soon as we see an opening," I whisper, "we'll make a break for it."

IT'S ALL UP TO KEVYN NOW!

GREETINGS, DOG BREATH!

ARE YOU CHAPS **BORED**?

...OR DO YOU **ALWAYS** WEAR SUCH DULL EXPRESSIONS?

GRRRRRR

GRRRR

IT'S WORKING! LET'S GO!

BUT SUPPOSE THE DOGS **CATCH** HIM!

THEY WON'T! LOOK!

CATS HAVE MAD CLIMBING SKILLS!

With Kevyn safe, we descend into the quarry. It's not hard to avoid being seen. The guards aren't expecting anything, and there are plenty of rocks to hide behind.

BUT WHERE ARE OUR PARENTS?

NO SIGN OF 'EM SO FAR.

WELL, IF THEY'VE BEEN PRISONERS FOR TEN YEARS, WE MIGHT NOT EVEN **RECOGNIZE** THEM!

Then we luck out. Two guards are standing within earshot. "I think the troublemaker has been in there long enough," the larger one grunts.

The smaller guard trudges into an opening in the rock face. When he returns a few moments later with a prisoner, a jolt of energy shoots through my body.

He's in chains. His tattered clothes hang off his body. And he's hairier than a barber's trash bin. But it's him, all right.

"Have you learned your lesson, you piece of rubbish?" the big guard rasps. "Don't try to lead a prisoners' revolt . . ."

Wait, he organized a prisoners' revolt? I feel my chest swell with pride. Our father's a REBEL!

"Now get back to work," the guard continues.

"Yes, we have," Mary says. "A COUPLE days, actually."

Clayton can't wrap his head around it all. "But how—?"

"I promise we'll explain later," I assure him.

Uh-oh. Looks like the klunkhounds were only the junior varsity. Here comes the A-Team.

"It's a MINEMOLE!" Simon hollers.

Mary races over to the guards. They're still cackling like wild hyenas. She grabs one of their spears.

"That won't work! Its coat is made of iron!" Perrin cries.

WE MUST TARGET ITS NOSE INSTEAD!

ITS NOSE? WHY?

MINEMOLES ARE **BLIND!** THEY HUNT BY SENSE OF **SMELL!**

LOOK OUT!

ROARR!

The creature snatches Perrin off the ground with a swipe of its paw. There's not a second to lose.

MILLIE! MAKE A FIRE!

A FIRE? NOW?

JUST **DO IT!!**

OKAY!

POOF!

Clayton can't wipe the dazed expression from his face. "You people are . . . are . . ."

I finish his sentence. "We're the Midknights. Now let's get out of here before the magic wears off."

I feel my cheeks go warm—I should have thought of that. Millie magically duplicates the guard's keys, and we dash around the quarry, unlocking each and every shackle.

Clayton shakes his head in amazement. "A talking cat! That would be the most surprising part of most days ..."

Mary and I ride in silence—which is weird. It's the first chance we've had to talk to our father, to tell him who we are, to tell him EVERYTHING . . .

SO WHY **DON'T** WE?

Good question. All I know is, I just don't feel ready. And maybe HE doesn't, either. The guy just spent ten years hacking brimstone out of the ground.

MAYBE HE JUST WANTS TO **CHILL**.

WHAT ARE YOUR NAMES, LADIES?

SNORT! **LADIES?**

SHE'S MARY. I'M MAX.

IT'S AN HONOR TO MEET YOU BOTH.

There's a long pause before he speaks again. "Earlier, you promised to explain all this," he says. "So I'll ask the same question my wife posed that night in the shack."

WHO **ARE** YOU GIRLS?

WELL, IT'S SORT OF COMPLICATED...

SSSSSSSSSSSSS

"Er . . . what's that noise?" Sedgewick asks.

"We've arrived at the place where my dear Emeline is imprisoned," Clayton answers. "The Blistering Bay."

"Yes, the water is scalding hot," Clayton confirms. "To touch it is to die."

"But then . . . where's the princess?" Mary asks.

He points at a tiny speck far across the bubbling surface. "On that island."

Clayton smiles sadly. "King Rotgut has enlisted many dark sorcerers to curse the air above these waters. No flying creature—not even a dragon—could survive it."

"Then we'll find a boat!" Kevyn counters. "One rugged enough to withstand the heat!"

Our father sighs. "Where would we find such a vessel?"

"AHOY!" whoops a familiar voice.

"Sing 'em aboard, boys!" Cap'n Scab bellows as we make our way up a wobbly plank and onto the *Scurvy Dog*.

"Slobberin' sea bass!" the pirate roars. "You've magically DOUBLED yourself!"

Cap'n Scab's jaw nearly hits the deck. "Shiver me liver!" he croaks, gaping at Kevyn. "He's a LAD, he is!"

CAN I INTEREST YOU IN A JOB AS A CABIN BOY?

GOOD HEAVENS, NO.

CAP'N, WHAT ARE YOU **DOING** HERE?

THE BLISTERING BAY DOESN'T SEEM LIKE PRIMO PIRATING TERRITORY!

"Right you are, Max, but I'm here for the health benefits!" Scab explains. "This place does wonders for my skin!"

THE STEAM REALLY OPENS UP THE PORES!

UH... THAT'S GREAT. WHEN YOU'RE DONE WITH THAT...

...CAN YOU TAKE US TO THAT ISLAND OUT THERE?

"Anything for you, Max!" he replies, steering the *Scurvy Dog* away from the shoreline. "But why would you travel to such a forsaken spot?"

"To rescue someone," I tell him. "The princess of Klunk."

"Sufferin' squid! A PRINCESS, you say?"

Mary and I join Clayton by the railing. He stares out over the frothing waves at the island in the distance.

"For ten long years, I've dreamed of finding my Emeline again," he says.

"Right," I reply. "Well, like we started to say before . . . it's complicated."

"Stop, stop!" Clayton chuckles, and I notice he has a kind laugh. "One at a time!"

Mary taps my shoulder. "You first."

Oh, no. I forgot it was a snap spell that trapped Gastley in the locket!

If Gastley's surprised to find himself in the middle of Blistering Bay, he doesn't show it. Instead, he lunges toward one of Scab's crewmen.

Gastley's beady eyes dart around the deck. When he sees me, a wicked grin crawls across his face.

"THERE'S the meddling imp I'm looking for!" he hisses. "Now, where were we when last we met?"

IF THERE'S TO BE A DUEL ON MY SHIP, YOU MUST ABIDE BY **PIRATE RULES!**

"Both sides must be armed!" Scab yaps, handing me a blade to match Gastley's. "And neither side can accept help!"

NOT **FIGHTING** HELP...

...OR **MAGICAL** HELP!

RATS.

In other words, Millie can't step in and turn Gastley into a wombat. But that's fine with me.

I'LL BEAT HIM FAIR AND SQUARE!

READY... SET...

DUEL!

SMACK!

OW!

Leave it to Gastley to fight dirty. He catches me on the side of my head with the flat of his sword. But I shake it off.

We battle back and forth. And I gotta give Gastley some credit: he's a decent fighter.

I'LL DESTROY YOU WITH MY BARE HANDS!

Gastley charges across the deck in a murderous rage. And me? I do what any knight would do in this situation.

"Thus endeth the cruel life of Gastley the Gruesome," Kevyn announces as we gaze down at the rippling waves.

I can't help but feel a little guilty. "I was just trying to trip the guy," I say, "not KILL him!"

"You didn't kill him," Perrin assures me.

GASTLEY WAS A VICTIM OF HIS OWN EVIL INSTINCTS.

LET ME SEE WHERE HE WHACKED YOU, MAX.

HMM... YOU HAVE A BUMP ON YOUR HEAD, BUT NO HARM DONE.

THANKS.

CRUNCH!

WHAT WAS **THAT**?

ER... LAND HO.

"That's not just any ship," Perrin notes. "Look at its flag."

Huh? Wonder what THAT'S all about. Clayton didn't even KNOW Millie until a few hours ago. He whispers something in her ear, and she nods in agreement.

We watch Clayton drop from the prow of the ship and land lightly on the island. He's unarmed. What's he DOING?

"Where is Emeline?" we hear him demand.

Rotgut smirks. "That's for me to know . . ."

The soldiers freeze. I don't think they're used to hearing sass from their potential victims.

Clayton points at the *Scurvy Dog.* "I have a friend over there who's a very gifted sorceress," he says, "and I just asked her to cast a spell . . ."

We look down the shoreline. Sure enough, Rotgut's ship is dropping faster than a rock in a bathtub.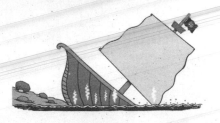

"That means the only way for you to get off the island is on OUR boat," Clayton continues, "which is home to a crew of bloodthirsty buccaneers!"

"Unless you believe you can defeat those cutthroats in combat," Clayton tells the soldiers . . .

It happens so fast, I almost miss it: Clayton decks Rotgut with one punch. The king of Klunk is flat on his back, out cold.

"Where is the princess?" Clayton asks one of the soldiers, and the man points at a nearby ridge.

That stops him. He waves us over to join him, and we fling ourselves off the ship. When we catch up near the top of the ridge, he greets us with a warm smile.

"It's a family reunion," he says, his eyes twinkling.

"When did you figure it out?" Mary asks.

Over the ridge, we come to a cave blocked by an iron gate. A key hangs on a peg nearby. Our dad slips the key into the lock, and the gate swings open with a harsh creak.

From inside the cave come sounds of movement. Then a woman steps unsteadily into the light. She's filthy. Her dress is torn. She's reed-thin, and her skin is as pale and brittle as a scrap of parchment.

"Wow," Mary whispers.

"I knew you'd find me," she says to Clayton.

"Look who ELSE I found," he tells her.

Her eyes open in wonder. Then they fill with tears. "Oh, my girls," she cries.

The four of us share a long hug. Then our mom glances back at the dark mouth of the cave.

"I'm ready to leave here now," she says firmly.

We walk slowly down the hill to the shoreline. The pirates are marching Rotgut's men onto the ship.

"Ahoy, Max! Perfect timing!" Cap'n Scab shouts. "We're just about ready to take these soldiers back to Klunk!"

"We can't just throw him overboard," our dad says. "Then we'd be as bad as HE is."

"I've got an idea," I announce.

"No," she declares, shaking her head. "I don't want to be queen. The people of Klunk should choose their own leaders. And I want to go somewhere new—for a fresh start."

"I know just the place," I tell her. I hurry over to Cap'n Scab, who's steering the *Scurvy Dog* into open waters.

"Chart a course, Cap'n!" I say. "As soon as we've dropped off these soldiers in Klunk . . ."

Epilogue

I'VE GOT THE EAR WAX BLUUUUUES!

WOW. JUST... WOW.

AND THIS IS ONE OF HIS **BETTER** SONGS!

IS IT TRUE HE'S GOING TO PERFORM AT THE CEREMONY TOMORROW?

YUP.

WHAT CEREMONY?

KING CONRAD IS MAKING OUR DAD A **KNIGHT**!

YEAH, AND YOU'RE ALL INVITED!

OOH! SHOULD WE WEAR FANCY CLOTHES?

WE'RE GOING TO! MAX AND I ARE WEARING **DRESSES**!

UGH. I LOOK AWFUL IN A DRESS.

I DOUBT THAT.

GREETINGS, MIDKNIGHTS!

HI, MUMBLIN!

I'D LIKE YOU TO MEET THE NEWEST RESIDENT OF SHADY ACRES!

TROTWELL!

EH? WHO'S THAT? MY EYESIGHT'S NOT WHAT IT USED TO BE!

WE WERE THERE THE NIGHT YOU SAVED PRINCESS EMELINE'S DAUGHTERS!

WERE YOU? MY, MY!

ER... WHATEVER HAPPENED TO THE BABY YOU TOOK TO GOBSMACK?

I LEFT HER WITH A **TROUBADOUR** WHO WAS PASSING THROUGH!

A **HORRIBLE** SINGER, BUT HE HAD A FRIENDLY FACE!

✳CHUCKLE!✳ THERE'S A MEMORABLE QUOTE FOR MY NEXT BOOK!

BOOK? KEVYN, YOU'RE AN **AUTHOR?**

AND A LIBRARIAN!

INDEED! MY FAVORITE PART OF THIS STORY...

...IS THAT MAX'S **LIBRARY CARD** PLAYED SUCH A PIVOTAL ROLE!

HEY, LOOK!

YOUR PARENTS AND PERRIN ARE GETTING A V.I.P. TOUR OF BYJOVIA!

I THINK WE'LL JOIN THEM!

SEE YOU LATER, GUYS!

AHEM! YOU'VE GOT A LITTLE CRUSH ON SEDGEWICK, DON'T YOU?

ER... MMMMAYBE.

BUT I'M TOO YOUNG TO HAVE A BOYFRIEND. AND TOO **BUSY**. I'VE GOT A LOT ON MY PLATE.

YEAH, LIKE GETTING TO KNOW OUR **PARENTS**.

EXACTLY. I'M STILL NOT SURE WHAT TO **CALL** THEM!

PLUS, I WANT PERRIN TO LIVE WITH US— I MEAN, IF THAT'S WHAT SHE WANTS.

AND UNCLE BUDRICK, TOO!

WOW. THERE'S SO MUCH STUFF TO FIGURE OUT.

UH-HUH. BUT YOU KNOW WHAT'S GREAT ABOUT IT?

Lincoln Peirce is a *New York Times* bestselling author and cartoonist. His comic strip *Big Nate*, featuring the adventures of an irrepressible sixth grader, appears in over 400 newspapers worldwide and online at gocomics.com/bignate. In 2010, he began a series of illustrated novels based on the strip, introducing Nate and his cast of classmates and teachers to a new generation of young readers. Now over twenty million Big Nate books have been sold, and Nickelodeon has created an animated series inspired by the self-styled "king of detention."

Max and the Midknights and *Max and the Midknights: Battle of the Bodkins*, Lincoln's instant *New York Times* bestselling novels for Crown Books for Young Readers, originated as a spoof of sword and sorcery tales. He later rewrote the story with a new and memorable protagonist: Max, a ten-year-old apprentice troubadour who dreams of becoming a knight. *The Tower of Time* reunites Max and her friends for a rollicking time-travel saga, supported by hundreds of dynamic illustrations employing the language of comics. Of the lively visual format that has become his trademark, Lincoln says, "I try to write the sorts of books I would have loved reading when I was a kid."

When he is not writing or drawing, Lincoln enjoys playing ice hockey, doing crossword puzzles, and hosting a weekly radio show devoted to vintage country music. He and his wife, Jessica, have two children and live in Portland, Maine.

Hey, *Max & the Midnights* readers! Be sure to check out the newest titles in Lincoln Peirce's *New York Times* bestselling Big Nate series.

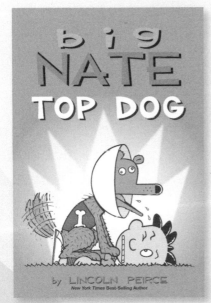

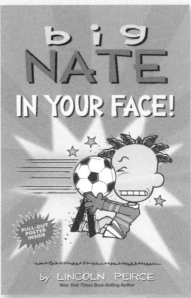

Andrews McMeel
PUBLISHING®
www.andrewsmcmeel.com